Alexandra
the Royal Baby Fairy

To my amazing mum, with all the love in the world

Special thanks to
Sarah Levison

ORCHARD BOOKS
338 Euston Road, London NW1 3BH
Orchard Books Australia
Level 17/207 Kent Street, Sydney, NSW 2000
A Paperback Original

First published in 2013 by Orchard Books

HiT entertainment

A CIP catalogue record for this book is available
from the British Library.

ISBN 978 1 40832 975 7

1 3 5 7 9 10 8 6 4 2

Printed in Great Britain

The paper and board used in this paperback are natural recyclable
products made from wood grown in sustainable forests. The
manufacturing processes conform to the environmental regulations
of the country of origin.

Orchard Books is a division of Hachette Children's Books,
an Hachette UK company

www.hachette.co.uk

Alexandra
the Royal Baby
Fairy

by Daisy Meadows

ORCHARD

www.rainbowmagic.co.uk

The Fairyland
Palace

Seeing Pool

Royal Nursery

NORWOOD
PALACE

Throne Room

Jack Frost's Ice Castle

Wetherbury Village

Aha! What's that I hear?
A 'precious bundle' will soon be near.
I think I'll take it for my own,
And keep it in my icy home!

A royal baby was a surprise,
But a good one, I now realise.
I'll teach it to play tricks on fairykind,
And Fairyland will soon be mine!

Contents

The Royal Palace

"Are we nearly there, Mum?" asked Kirsty, leaning as far forwards in the car as her seatbelt would let her. "We can't wait to get to the palace!"

Mrs Tate turned her head a little to smile at Kirsty and her best friend, Rachel Walker, who were sitting side by side in the back of the car. "Not long now, girls. When we reach the top of this hill you'll be able to see Norwood Palace straight ahead. Look, there it is!"

The girls gasped as they saw the palace
through the windows of the car.
The regal building nestled in a lush
green valley. It was built from golden
stone that glistened warmly in the
spring sunshine. A long driveway curved
round to the front of the palace, and
tall, elegant pillars stood by the grand

entrance doors. The girls could see beautiful formal gardens stretching out all around the palace.

"It's amazing!" cried Rachel as the car pulled into the drive. "Just think of all the kings, queens, princes and princesses who have lived here."

Rachel Walker was staying with her best friend Kirsty Tate for the spring half term holidays. The girls had been really looking forward to visiting Norwood Palace, a beautiful place near Wetherbury. Mrs Tate was a volunteer at the palace and today the girls were going to help with a special children's open day.

Not only were Kirsty and Rachel best friends, they were also great friends with the Rainbow Magic fairies!

Ever since the two girls had met on Rainspell Island, they had been lucky enough to have lots of amazing, magical adventures. They couldn't wait to meet more fairy friends, but wise Queen Titania, queen of the fairies, had once told the girls that they had to wait for the magic to come to them!

Mrs Tate parked at the side of the palace and opened the car door for Rachel and Kirsty. "OK, girls," she smiled, "I'll be based in the royal kitchens today and you'll be right at the top of the house in the old royal nursery. It's lovely up there, with lots of interesting toys and books to look at. I'm sure the visiting children will really enjoy seeing where royal babies and children used to sleep and play."

Mrs Tate handed the girls a folder containing a map of the palace, some interesting facts about the royal nursery and some quizzes and colouring pages for the visitors. "I'll come and see how you're getting on in an hour or so," she said. "You've got snacks and drinks in your backpacks."

"Great, thanks Mum," smiled Kirsty, grabbing Rachel's hand and running up the stairs into the palace. They couldn't wait to explore!

The girls quickly made their way up the grand staircase to the first floor of the palace. There were lots of paintings and tapestries on the walls and they glimpsed precious vases and ornaments in each of the rooms they passed. The girls raced along the wide corridors and soon they reached another, smaller set of stairs leading right up to the top of the palace.

"Can you imagine growing up here?" asked Rachel, smiling at Kirsty. "Think of all the fun you'd have playing hide-and-seek, or tag. Wow!"

The girls had reached the top of the stairs and were now in the royal nursery. Because they were up under the roof of the palace the ceiling was sloped, making the room feel very cosy. The sun shone in through the slanted windows, causing the light to dance magically in the air. The room was decorated in soft pink and blue stripes and two ornate cots with floaty canopies were in the centre of the room.

Pretty pictures of animals hung on the walls and toys of all shapes and sizes sat on the shelves along the sides of the room. A toybox was full of games and cuddly toys.

"This doll is amazing!" cried Rachel, carefully picking up a china doll wearing a delicate lace gown. "She looks just like Kate the Royal Wedding Fairy!"

"And look at all the brilliant books," said Kirsty, picking up a book called *Fairy Stories from Around the World.*

"Although I'm sure *our* magical adventures with the fairies are just as exciting as the ones in here!"

As Kirsty closed the book a cloud of dust flew up into the air and hovered just above the girls' heads. But rather than fading away, the dust seemed to get thicker and sparkled mysteriously. The girls exchanged an excited glance – this looked like fairy magic!

Alexandra Appears!

The cloud of dust formed a glistening whirlwind and then a tiny little fairy appeared from the top, spinning round and round like a model fairy in a musical box!

"Hello, girls!" she cried, waving her wand and making the sparkling dust whirlwind disappear. "I'm Alexandra the Royal Baby Fairy."

Alexandra was wearing a beautiful pink dress with sparkly gems and a silk bow at the waist. Red ballet pumps glistened on her tiny feet. She had wavy auburn hair that was loosely fastened with a sparkly hairclip and a pretty pendant glistened around her neck.

"Hello, Alexandra!" chorused the girls. How exciting it was to meet a new fairy friend.

"Oh, it's so nice to be back here!" smiled Alexandra, zooming up into the air and flying a loop-the-loop.

"Victoria and James, the royal babies who used to live here, were *so* adorable."

"Do you look after all royal babies, Alexandra?" asked Rachel.

"I do," smiled Alexandra, looking dreamily around the beautiful nursery. But then her little face fell. "Oh," she sighed. "It's so nice to meet you both and be back at the palace that I almost forgot why I'm here!"

"Oh, no!" said Kirsty, as Alexandra landed on her shoulder. "What's the matter?"

"Well, whenever a new royal baby arrives I am *always* there to greet them," explained Alexandra, sitting down on Kirsty's shoulder. "I give each adorable baby my magical silver rattle to hold for a few moments, and this makes sure that the royal baby has a wonderful childhood and is destined to enjoy all of their royal duties."

"Is it your magical object that's missing?" asked Rachel.

Alexandra gave a sad smile.

"Thankfully the rattle is safe, for Queen Titania is looking after it. You see, girls, it's not my magical rattle that's missing. It's the new royal baby!"

Kirsty and Rachel gasped.

"That's terrible!" cried Kirsty.

"It is!" agreed Alexandra. "Princess Grace and Prince Arthur, whom you met when you helped Kate the Royal Wedding Fairy, were expecting their bundle of royal baby joy to be delivered by Foster, the head stork. He collects all Fairyland babies from the Magical Gooseberry Bush and delivers them safely to their parents. But he's gone missing on the way back from collecting the royal baby and we're all very worried."

"Can we help?" asked Rachel immediately.

"Oh, I do hope so, girls!" cried Alexandra. "Will you come to Fairyland with me? I know you have an important job to do here at the palace, but time will stand still whilst you're away."

"Of course we will!" chorused the girls at the same time. They were not going to let down their fairy friends.

Alexandra waved her wand and a glittering whirlwind appeared. It surrounded the two girls and Rachel and Kirsty felt themselves growing smaller and smaller, with gossamer wings

upon their backs.
Within seconds,
they touched
down
outside the
Fairyland
Palace and
the girls
saw lots
of familiar
fairy faces. There was Princess Grace
and Prince Arthur, and Kate the Royal
Wedding Fairy. They spotted their dear
friend Ruby the Red Fairy, standing
next to Elizabeth the Jubilee Fairy. At
the very front of the group were wise
King Oberon and kind Queen Titania,
rulers of Fairyland. The girls curtseyed to
the king and queen.

"Rachel and Kirsty, we are very pleased to see you," said King Oberon, his kind eyes serious. "Thank you for coming to help us once again. We have created a Seeing Pool to find out what has happened to Foster and his precious bundle."

The girls and Alexandra joined the
fairies around the Seeing Pool. The scene
showed a beautiful white stork landing
by a large gooseberry bush. A glowing
light surrounded the bush and each
of its beautiful red berries. The leaves
parted and a tightly wrapped bundle was
lowered carefully to the floor. The fairies
looking at the Seeing Pool gasped; out of
the blanket peeped a
tiny face framed
by perfect
curls.
Foster
carefully
picked up
the baby
bundle and
took to the air.

After a few minutes of flying above Fairyland, Foster suddenly slowed down. The Seeing Pool showed that a strange creature on the ground had attracted the stork's attention. It had wings made from scruffy feathers and a very large beak, and it seemed to be covered in a tatty white sheet. Foster landed beside the strange creature to see if it needed any help.

Suddenly, the creature pulled off the sheet and tore off the fake beak, and Jack Frost was revealed! The mean Ice Lord cackled loudly, grabbed Foster and his precious bundle and muttered a spell. A large ice bolt appeared and Jack Frost jumped onto it, clinging to Foster and the royal baby. Then, in a blue flash, they were gone. The Seeing Pool clouded over.

The assembled fairies looked shocked.

"I can't believe it!" fumed Alexandra the Royal Baby Fairy. "Of all the mean, horrible tricks to play. *Why* would Jack Frost want Foster and the royal baby?"

Kirsty and Rachel exchanged a glance.

"There's only one thing to do," said Kirsty with a determined look on her face. "We're going to have to visit the Ice Castle and find out what Jack Frost is up to!"

To the Rescue!

"Goodbye, everyone!" called Rachel, Kirsty and Alexandra to their fairy friends, as they set off to the Ice Castle.

After flying through the sky for a little while the three friends spotted the towering turrets of Jack Frost's home. Tendrils of icy cold mist curled around their wings as they landed behind a snow-covered pine tree, close to the front doors of the castle.

"I can see quite a few goblin guards," warned Alexandra.

"You're right," said Rachel, peering around the side of the tree. "But there's an open window on the left-hand side of the castle. Let's sneak round and fly through it."

The three fairies carefully made their way around the castle and flew up and through the open window.

Luckily the silly goblin guards didn't spot them, as the horrid creatures were too busy bragging about who had the longest, dirtiest toenails. Yuck!

The friends didn't spot anything in the large store cupboard they landed in, so they quickly flew out into the corridor.

"Alexandra, will you be able to sense when the royal baby is nearby?" asked Kirsty, peeping her head round the door of a room filled with nothing but ice-blue outfits.

"I think so," said Alexandra, "although we'll *all* be able to hear the baby if the poor little darling is unhappy. Even fairy babies can cry very loudly!"

"Hang on, I do hear something," said Rachel suddenly, pausing in mid air. "But it sounds more like squawking than crying."

The squawking came from behind huge double doors, which Kirsty and Rachel recognised as leading to Jack Frost's grand Throne Room. The friends eased their way into the room through a crack in the door.

The Throne Room was empty except for a huge, spiky throne at one end. Above the throne, hanging from one of the roof beams, was a small cage, and squashed in the cage was a large white bird with black markings and big, sad eyes.

"Foster!" Alexandra cried, flying straight up to the cage. "Oh, you poor thing! What happened? Where is the royal baby? These are my friends Kirsty and Rachel, and we've come to rescue you both!"

"Oh, Alexandra," sniffed Foster. "I'm so glad to see you. I've been so worried!"

"Can you tell us what happened, Foster?" asked Rachel. "Do you know why Jack Frost took the royal baby? That might help us work out where the baby is now."

37

"It's all a terrible mistake!" whimpered the poor bird. "You see, Jack Frost didn't know that I was carrying a *baby* in my bundle. The nosy thing was spying on some fairies and he overheard them talking about how precious and special my delivery would be. He thought I was carrying gold or fairy treasure! When he realised it was a baby he wasn't sure what to do."

"Do you know where he took the baby?" asked Kirsty urgently.

"No," replied the stork sadly. "He shut me in this cage as soon as we got back here. At first he seemed cross but then he started laughing and dancing around the room with the baby. He muttered something about really teaching the fairies a lesson this time."

Alexandra waved
her wand and
the lock on
the cage
burst open.

"Foster,
you must be
very tired. Fly
straight back to
the palace now and let the
king and queen know you are all right."

"I will, but I'll come back soon!" cried
Foster, stretching his wings and flying
shakily out of the window.

The three fairy friends set off to search
the rest of the castle.

"It's strange that we haven't seen many
goblins yet," called Kirsty. "Perhaps they
are with the royal baby."

39

The three fairies made their way down a flight of winding stairs. As they looked around, deciding which of the rooms to search next, they heard a thud and a shriek coming from one of the rooms.

"That definitely sounded like a goblin!" cried Alexandra, pointing to a big door straight ahead.

"Let's see what's going on," said Kirsty and the three friends peered through the door.

In front of them was a *very* strange sight. There were at least seven goblins in

the room, forming a semicircle. All were
doing different things; one was juggling,
one was stuffing bogmallows into its
mouth and another was drawing pictures
on a blackboard. In the middle of the
floor, lying fast asleep and wrapped in
a soft yellow blanket, was the beautiful
royal baby.

Goblin Teachers

"Oh, thank goodness!" cried Alexandra, clasping her little hands together. The Royal Baby Fairy started to fly towards the baby but Rachel grabbed her arm.

"Alexandra, we mustn't let the goblins see us! They'll try to catch us. I think we should sneak in and hide until we know what their plans are for the royal baby."

"You're right," agreed Alexandra, her little wings drooping. "I just wanted to give the sweet little baby a cuddle and then get it back to Princess Grace and Prince Arthur. But we must be careful with all these tricksy goblins around."

The three friends waited patiently. When the two goblins closest to them started squabbling, the fairies flew into the room, staying close to the floor. They hid behind an armchair in the corner of the room, making sure  they had a good view of the royal baby.

The plump goblin, who had been

stuffing lots of bogmallows into his mouth, gave a huge belch. "Silly baby!" he moaned. "I've been showing it how to eat bogmallows for ages now and the rude little thing won't even wake up and pay attention. This is *so* boring!"

"I know," nodded the goblin by the blackboard, throwing a piece of chalk on the floor. "Look at all the brilliant pictures I've drawn showing how to play the best tricks. The ungrateful little creature hasn't even looked!"

"Stop whingeing," screeched a tall
goblin with a large wart on his nose.
"The boss said we had to teach this little
thing how to be sneaky. Then, when
it grows up, we'll use it to play extra-
specially mean tricks on the fairies!"

Behind the armchair the three fairies gasped. So *that* was why Jack Frost had decided to keep the little fairy baby. He was planning on making the baby part of his sneaky goblin gang!

All of a sudden, the baby opened its eyes and looked around. It gave a small whimper, and then a louder cry. Then the cry turned into a howl!

"Do something," cried one of the goblins, clasping his hands to his ears. "Make it stop!"

All of the goblins seemed scared of the royal baby. The warty goblin rolled a bogmallow towards it, but of course the little one didn't respond. Another goblin started to juggle balls of mud close to the baby's head, but that made it cry even harder.

"Oh, I can't stand it any more!" cried Alexandra. And before Kirsty or Rachel could stop her, the plucky little fairy flew straight into the middle of the goblin circle. The girls were right behind her – they knew friends had to stick together.

"Arghhhh! Where did you horrible bunch come from?" cried the goblins, leaping backwards and looking all around them as if they expected hundreds of fairies to appear.

"You should be ashamed of yourselves!" shouted Alexandra. She was so angry that she wasn't at all frightened of the goblins. "This precious baby should be with its mummy and daddy, not with you silly creatures."

The goblins looked very sorry. "We didn't mean to make it upset," one of them whined, hanging his head. "It just doesn't act like a goblin baby!"

"Well, of course it doesn't," scolded Alexandra. "That's because this is a fairy baby, a *royal* fairy baby!" She smiled down at the little bundle, who had stopped crying and was gazing peacefully up at Alexandra with big, beautiful eyes. "How would you like it if a little goblin baby was kept away from its mummy and daddy?"

Rachel and Kirsty heard a strange glugging sound. They looked around and realised that several of the goblins were crying!

"We *were* being nice to it!" sobbed the plump goblin. "I even tried to give it one of my bogmallows!"

Alexandra stopped frowning and looked at the goblins kindly. "I know you were trying your best. But this baby needs to be with fairies, not goblins! I'm going to take the little one to its rightful home." And with that, Alexandra started to fly towards the baby.

"Oh, I don't think so!" said an icy voice from outside, and suddenly poor Alexandra was frozen in mid-flight by a bolt of magic. The room grew much colder as Jack Frost appeared in the doorway.

An Icy Time

"Well, well, well. What have we here?"
sneered the Ice Lord, striding into the
centre of the room and towering over the
royal baby and poor, frozen Alexandra.
"I knew it was only a matter of time
before you interfering girls would turn
up. Well, it's time to teach you a lesson
once and for all!" Jack Frost pointed
his wand straight at the girls, who felt
themselves begin to freeze.

But then the little fairy baby slowly stretched its tiny wings and flew straight towards Jack Frost! The icy magic flowing from his wand stopped suddenly as the royal baby flew into his arms and snuggled close to him!

Jack Frost looked at the baby, amused. Rachel and Kirsty shook their wings to warm them up. "Let's see if we can help Alexandra whilst Jack Frost is distracted by the baby," whispered Kirsty. The girls flew over to Alexandra, but the poor little fairy was frozen stiff. "We'll have to see if we can persuade Jack Frost to undo his spell," said Rachel, determined to help their fairy friend.

As the two girls turned back to the Ice Lord they noticed something very strange. The mean creature was smiling at the little baby in his arms, and cooing in an adoring way!

"Who is a cute little fairy-wairy?" Jack Frost muttered. "You are, yes, you are. Hey diddly-doo, Uncle Jack loves you!"

As the Ice Lord bent over the royal baby, a tiny chubby hand reached out and grabbed Jack Frost's wand. The baby waved it in the air and icy particles of magic started to shoot from the wand, heading off in all directions! One of them hit the goblin by the blackboard and he shrank to the size of a mouse and started shrieking crossly in a high-pitched voice.

Another goblin became frozen stiff in a giant icicle and two goblins standing close together were trapped in the middle of a large snowball with just their arms and legs poking out.

Luckily, one of the magical sparks hit Alexandra, causing the freezing spell to wear off. She immediately flew towards the girls.

"Look, Alexandra," said Kirsty, "Jack Frost is being very nice to the baby!"

Jack Frost had managed to get his wand back from the royal baby and was now singing a nursery rhyme.

"I'm *so* glad the precious little one is OK," said Alexandra, "but how are we going to get the baby back from Jack Frost? It looks like he's enjoying himself!"

"I've got an idea," said Rachel thoughtfully. "What if we try to make Jack Frost understand how much hard work it will be to look after the baby? And explain that it will be a long time before the little fairy will be able to play any tricks?"

"That's a great idea, Rachel!" said Kirsty. "And I think I know what to say to persuade him." Kirsty whispered her idea to Rachel and Alexandra and the three friends flew towards Jack Frost.

The Ice Lord scowled at the fairies as they approached him. "Go away!" he snapped. "Can't you see I'm busy?"

"Oh, *this* isn't busy," said Alexandra with a big smile. "The baby will need to be fed soon, and then its nappy will need changing, and this will happen several times a day. And it will wake up lots at night too, so you won't get much sleep. But you won't mind the sleepless nights, will you?"

Jack Frost turned a paler shade of blue. "Sleepless nights?" he muttered. "But I need my beauty sleep. I get very grumpy if I don't have at least twelve hours' rest a night!" And he looked at the little baby with a frown.

"You're *so* good with the baby and the sweet little thing obviously really likes you," said Rachel soothingly. "But *this* little one is going to need lots of looking after for a very long time. How about if you had another baby to play with, one that's easier to look after?"

"Hmm, well, that does sound like *quite* a good idea," said Jack Frost, looking around him at the chaos the baby had caused. He glared at the fairies suspiciously. "But where is this other baby? How do I know you're not playing tricks on me?"

Alexandra smiled at the Ice Lord. "The new baby is outside. Let's go and meet it."

The three fairies and Jack Frost headed outside to the frozen pond. Jack Frost was holding onto the royal baby tightly. He certainly wasn't going to give it up easily!

"You lied!" screeched the icy creature, looking all around him. "There are no babies here. I'm keeping this one!"

"Wait, look over there!" cried Alexandra, pointing at the horizon. The girls and Jack Frost looked at the sky and saw a shape coming towards them... but what was it?

A Royal Delivery

The girls quickly realised that a beautiful
white bird was flying towards them. It
was Foster, carrying a new baby bundle!
The stork landed by a flock of snow
geese, near the pond and one snow goose
immediately came forward; it was Jack
Frost's precious pet. Then out of the
bundle waddled a gorgeously fluffy snow
goose chick.

"Oh! My precious snow goose had a baby!" cried the Ice Lord, jumping up and down with joy. He quickly handed over the royal baby to Alexandra and ran over to greet the snow goose chick.

"Hello, little darling!" murmured Alexandra to the royal baby, who was looking up at her happily. "It's so nice to meet you at last."

Alexandra waved her wand in the air and chanted, "Now we're with the royal baby, let my magic rattle come to me!"

The air shimmered for a moment and then Alexandra's beautiful silver rattle appeared. She placed it in the hand of the royal baby and the tiny fairy shook it up and down.

A beautiful tinkling sound came from the rattle and a mist of magical sparkles surrounded the little one.

The baby gurgled contentedly, smiled at the three girls, and settled down to sleep.

"Hurrah!" cried Rachel and Kirsty excitedly, giving each other and Alexandra a huge hug.

"Now, let's leave this freezing place and take the baby back to the Fairyland Palace," said Alexandra. She looked over to where Jack Frost was cuddling the snow goose chick and smiled. "Who'd have thought that Jack Frost could be such a softie? Babies really do bring out the best in everyone!"

Foster picked up the sleeping baby in his beak and the friends took to the air again, flying towards the sparkling pink turrets of the palace. It was so nice to feel the sun on their wings after the icy mists of Jack Frost's domain!

As they approached the palace the fairies could see a large group gathered to greet them. There was King Oberon and Queen Titania, and Prince Arthur and Princess Grace, who were jumping

up and down with excitement. Jennifer
the Babysitter Fairy was also there
with a large group of fairy toddlers
and children, who were waving a
sparkly banner that read: 'Welcome
Home Your Highness!'

As the fairies and Foster landed, even
more fairies rushed out to say hello. But
the crowd parted to let Princess Grace
and Prince Arthur come to the front.
The royal couple had tears in their eyes
as Alexandra gave a deep curtsey and
handed over the royal baby to them.
The little fairy baby opened its eyes
and cooed happily at its mummy and
daddy. The watching fairies clapped and
cheered and with a wave of his royal
wand, King Oberon created amazing
fireworks that whizzed magically around
the dusky sky, bursting with every colour
of the rainbow!

"Dearest Rachel and Kirsty, how
can we ever thank you?" smiled
Queen Titania, putting an arm around
each girl.

"It was our pleasure," said Kirsty with a huge smile.

"We just love helping the fairies," added Rachel. "We'll be here to help *whenever* you need us!"

Before too long it was time for the girls to return to Norwood Palace. They hugged all of their friends goodbye and held hands as they were whizzed back to the royal nursery. No time at all had passed in the human world!

The first of the young visitors soon arrived and the girls were kept busy handing out information sheets and activity packs and showing the children all the fun things in the royal nursery.

"Phew, what an exciting day!" said Rachel as the two girls made their way down the palace staircase later that afternoon. "Oh look, there's your mum."

Mrs Tate was on her mobile phone, looking very happy. She finished her call and turned to the girls. "Hi there, girls! I've just had some very exciting news.

Kirsty, your lovely cousin Esther has had her baby! We're going to pop in and see them on the way home. I don't expect you girls will ever have seen such a tiny little baby."

As Mrs Tate walked ahead to the car, the two girls smiled at each other.

"Rachel, can you believe we will have managed to meet two new babies in one day?" whispered Kirsty.

"I know," smiled Rachel, squeezing her best friend's hand. "And to think one of them was a royal fairy baby! This really has been one of the most magical adventures ever!"

Now Kirsty and Rachel
must help...

Mae the Panda Fairy

Read on for a sneak peek...

Kirsty Tate gazed happily at the tall hedgerows, her bare arm resting on the open window as the car travelled along the bumpy country road. Pretty red, yellow and pink flowers were tangled among the green leaves. She could smell the tang of cut grass and the earthiness of freshly turned soil.

"We're nearly there, girls," said Mrs Tate from the driver's seat. "Look!"

She slowed the car and pointed to a signpost at the side of the winding road.

WILD WOODS NATURE RESERVE 2 MILES

Kirsty smiled at her best friend Rachel Walker, who was sitting beside her.

"I'm so excited," said Rachel. "The sun's shining, we've got all of the summer holidays stretching ahead of us, and a whole week to spend here with the animals."

It was the start of the summer holidays, and Kirsty and Rachel were on their way to Wild Woods, the local nature reserve. Rachel was staying with Kirsty, and their parents had arranged for them to spend every day that week there as volunteers. As the car turned up a rough, narrow track, their hearts were racing with anticipation.

"It's going to be amazing to be helping out as junior rangers," said Kirsty. "I can't wait to see the animals!"

At the end of the track was an archway, printed with green words:

WELCOME TO WILD WOODS

NATURE RESERVE

Mrs Tate drove through the archway and stopped the car next to a small wooden hut. The door of the hut opened and a tanned, dark-haired woman came out. She was wearing khaki shorts, a white shirt and walking boots, and she smiled and waved at them.

"Look, there's Becky," said Mrs Tate. "She's the head of Wild Woods."

Rachel and Kirsty jumped out of the car and Becky walked over to them.

"It's great to meet you both," said Becky, shaking their hands and smiling. "I'm really pleased that you're going to be spending this week with us. It's great to meet young people who are interested in conservation."

"We can't wait to get started!" said Rachel exitedly.

"I thought you should begin by going off on your own to explore the reserve," said Becky. "It's the best way to get a feel for it. I'll meet you back here this afternoon and give you your first task."

"That sounds like great fun!" chorused Kirsty and Rachel.

Read **Mae the Panda Fairy** to find out what adventures are in store for Kirsty and Rachel!

Meet the fairies, play games
and get sneak peeks at
the latest books!

www.rainbowmagicbooks.co.uk

There's fairy fun for everyone on
our wonderful website.
You'll find great activities, competitions, stories and
fairy profiles, and also a special newsletter.

Get 30% off all Rainbow Magic books at
www.rainbowmagicbooks.co.uk

Enter the code RAINBOW at the checkout.
Offer ends 31 December 2013.

Offer valid in United Kingdom and Republic of Ireland only.